PAPERBOY III

The School Of Doom

By

Omari Jeremiah

Illustrations by Bernie Rollins

MORTON BOOKS, Inc.

FIRST MORTON BOOKS EDITION
Copyright 2006, Omari Jeremiah

Morton ISBN:1-929188-10-2
Cover design by Bernie Rollins
www.robmorton.com

Printed in the United States of America

This book is dedicated to Aquisha Jeremiah, Mommy, Daddy, Osei, Skyla, Aunt Pat, Uncle Darryl, DJ, Gran-Gran, Chris, Julia and Ms. Holland. Thanks for your ideas and constant support.

Contents

A secret is discovered.

A new enemy approaches….

And an organization shows how strong it really is………

After the Mad Hunter was defeated, Paperboy returned to his home to find out he is linked to one of his enemies in a way he never imagined. Even more surprisingly, Paperboy and his friends are kidnapped and taken to a school completely controlled by LOEP (League of Evil People).

Can Paperboy and his friends escape this horrible school?
Or will they fall before LOEP's undiscovered strength?

Chapter 1

THE UNEXPECTED GUEST

ONE

The sun shone brightly as Michael played cards with James and Nina.

"One five," Michael declared as he played a card.

" One seven," James declared as he played a card.

"I win," Nina happily announced in a loud voice, as she played her last card.

"That's the eighth game in a row!" James exclaimed. "This is impossible!"

"I'm just too good." Nina said.

"I'm tired of playing cards," Michael said. "Let's try out the walkie-talkie system."

"Good idea," James said.

"No." Nina said, " We are going to keep playing until I lose."

Michael and James groaned. James had recently created a walkie-talkie system that would allow him, Michael and Nina to talk to each other as long as they were within 2 miles of each other. This project interested Michael and James, but not Nina. Nina was more interested in the card game she was playing with James and Michael. She had cheated throughout all the games she played and she was not ready to stop now.

It had been two weeks since Paperboy, James, and Nina fought the Mad Hunter. Ever since then, fewer bullies had been in the schoolyard. Michael was sure they were coming up with a plan to destroy him. Everyone was out to get him. Mr. Raptor wanted to capture him and everyone in LOEP wanted to destroy him. Michael was almost overwhelmed by his enemies until James and Nina helped him fight his enemies and bear the burden of being Paperboy.

Five minutes later the doorbell rang. Michael's mother answered the door.

"Who is it?" James asked.

Michael looked out his door as his mother opened the front door. Michael could not believe who was at the door. It was Mr. Raptor! Michael stepped back in surprise.

"Who is it?" James asked again.

"It... It's Mr. Raptor," Michael managed to say.

Nina and James looked up at him in disbelief. They put down the cards and walked over and looked out Michael's door. All three saw Mr. Raptor talking to Michael's mother, and they quickly backed into Michael's room.

"This can't be good," James uttered.

Michael took another quick peek out his room at Mr. Raptor. Why would Mr. Raptor be at his house?

"Michael!" Michael's mother called. Michael was scared to answer.

"Yes," He managed to say.

"Please come downstairs."

"Okay."

Michael looked worriedly at James and Nina. He then went downstairs to his mother. James and Nina watched from Michael's door.

"I should have told you this before," Michael's mother started. "But I didn't think you were ready. Now I feel you are ready. Michael, this is your father," Michael's mother said as she pointed to Mr. Raptor.

Michael couldn't believe it. This was his father? The person who wanted to capture him at any cost was his father? Michael stuttered and finally managed to speak.

"I... I don't know what to say," he said.

Mr. Raptor smiled and walked up to Michael. "It's all right." He said. "I know why you're surprised. You have seen me at PS 266, haven't you?"

"Yes. You have been trying to capture Paperboy."

"Yes, and I will succeed at capturing him," he said with pride. Little did Mr. Raptor know that Paperboy stood right in front of him.

"This is Scott who is your brother," Mr. Raptor said pointing to a neat dark skinned boy with black hair who was standing beside the door. This was another surprise Michael was not ready for. He had a brother!

"Hi." Scott said.

"Hi." Michael answered.

"You and Scott can get to know each other in your room, Michael," Michael's mother suggested.

Michael looked at Scott and said, "Follow me." Michael led Scott to his room. "Scott, this is Nina and James."

"Hi," Nina and James said in unison. Scott waved back.

"Want to play a card game?" Nina offered.

"Sure," Scott answered.

During the game, Michael, James, Nina, and Scott talked. Michael got to know his brother. He was a mild boy who liked to tell jokes and was always cheerful.

"So what school do you go to?" Nina asked.

"I'm... I'm not in school right now," Scott answered. Michael saw a little of Scott's cheerfulness disappear. Nina smiled and turned to Michael.

"It's like his school was taken over by LOEP," Nina said pointing to Scott. Nina turned to Scott.

"Sorry, you probably don't know about —"

"LOEP," Scott interrupted. Now all of Scott's cheerfulness was gone. It was replaced by anger. "LOEP took over my school."

Michael, James, and Nina gasped.

"What happened?" James asked.

Scott looked at the ceiling. He then took a deep breath.

"The school I used to go to was PS 244. It was a wonderful school, with great students, caring teachers, and a devoted principal. Then LOEP came along. They took over our school. They drove out the school guards, principal, teachers, and staff. They made us their prisoners. We were prisoners of our own school. The head of LOEP, a boy named Max Parker, would tell us to join LOEP or remain a prisoner of PS 244. Some people joined and some resisted LOEP. I resisted LOEP. I was, and still am, LOEP's greatest enemy. I escaped from PS 244 and from there I helped other prisoners escape. I entered and departed PS 244 everyday to help prisoners escape, and I never got caught. One time I ran into Max. I knew if I destroyed Max, I could get my old school back. I didn't destroy him, but I managed to leave a scar on his face. He has been furious ever since, and promises someday to return the favor."

"One day I was caught and I became a prisoner of PS 244 once again. I was held there for two months. Terrible things happened to me and other prisoners during that time. Shorty came to me one day and promised he would return the favor. I managed to escape the next day. My father had been looking for me. He said he would transfer me to his school, so he could keep an eye on me. Max Parker will pay for what he's done. He took away everything I loved about school. He still controls PS 244, and his organization has grown stronger. I don't know if I will ever see my school the way it used to be. But I do know that Max will pay for what he did. He will pay."

Michael, James, and Nina sat there stunned; tears in their eyes.

"Scott!" Mr. Raptor called.

Scott went to his father and left without saying goodbye to Michael, James, or Nina. Michael understood his brother now. And he knew what was going to happen when he came to PS 266. Scott would try to get revenge.

The next day Michael got up and started getting ready for school. He knew James, Nina, and Scott were getting ready at their homes too. Michael got up from his bed, stretched, took a shower, got dressed, made his breakfast, and then changed into his Paperboy costume. Paperboy rode his PaperMobile to P.S. 266. Once he arrived in school, he chained the PaperMobile to the gate and ran to PS 266. He quickly changed in the janitor's closet. Michael walked out of the janitor's closet and went to class.

During class an announcement came on the loudspeaker.

"Attention students and teachers. Please report to the playground area. We have a new student!"

The class groaned. Everyone made their way unto the playground. Outside, they gathered around the new student and the Principal. Michael saw that Scott had recovered his cheerfulness.

"This is Scott," Mr. Pride said. "Would you like to say anything, Scott?"

"No thanks," Scott answered.

"All right then. In that case, please return to class."

Everyone reluctantly returned to their classes. Miss Rex continued teaching her lesson. Half an hour later the bell rang for recess. Michael quickly walked out of class and into the janitor's closet to change. Paperboy then walked out of the janitor's closet and to the playground. Paperboy was armed with two paper airplanes, one on each hand between his pointer and middle fingers; two paper claws, one on each hand; two paper lasers, one on each of his two front pockets; and two Paper Blade Boomerangs (PBB), one on each hand between his middle and index finger.

In the playground, Paperboy saw no bullies. Paperboy knew something was wrong. Paperboy walked out to the middle of the playground. Suddenly, he saw the ScizzorMen climbing the gate into the playground. Paperboy was alarmed. Once the ScizzorMen were on the other side of the gate, they shouted,

"Paperboy!"

All of the kids looked at the ScizzorMen. Unfortunately, this included Scott. Scott recognized the ScizzorMen and started to get angry. Paperboy waited until the ScizzorMen saw him and walked up to them. ScizzorMan B cleared his throat.

"You're coming with us."

"Where?" Paperboy asked.

" Wherever we take you," ScizzorMan B answered.

"I don't think so."

Paperboy attacked ScizzorMan B with his paper airplane. Before ScizzorMan B could react to this attack Paperboy tripped him. Suddenly ScizzorMan A tackled Paperboy to the ground. ScizzorMan C aimed at Paperboy with a scissor gun. He then fired. Paperboy dodged the attack and got back up. ScizzorMan B got up also. ScizzorMan B tried to attack Paperboy with his scissors. Paperboy dodged it. ScizzorMan C then moved behind Paperboy, grabbed him, and held him still. Before Paperboy could use his Paper claw,

ScizzorMan A and B attacked him with their scissors.

All of a sudden ScizzorMan C was bound in ropes. Paperboy knew what happened to ScizzorMan C. He was caught in a protractor trap. Suddenly James appeared in his hockey mask and roller skates and attacked ScizzorMan A with his protractor.

"AHHHHHH!" ScizzorMan A cried out in pain. ScizzorMan B then kicked James and attacked fiercely with his scissors. These showers of attacks were more than James could handle and he fell to the ground. ScizzorMan A picked him up and held him still. Paperboy attacked ScizzorMan B with his paper airplane. ScizzorMan B dodged the attack and hit Paperboy with a powerful uppercut. Paperboy fell 5 feet back from ScizzorMan B. ScizzorMan B ran up to Paperboy and looked back at his brothers.

"What should we do?" he asked.

"Knock them out," ScizzorMan A suggested.

"Good idea," ScizzorMan B agreed.

ScizzorMan B raised his fist to Paperboy. Paperboy groaned and tried to get up. But before he could, ScizzorMan B struck. Suddenly everything in Paperboy's world went black.

"Did you kill him?"

"No."

Paperboy's eyes slowly opened.

"He's alive."

Paperboy saw the ScizzorMen looking at him.

"AHH!" Paperboy exclaimed. He jumped back in surprise. Paperboy looked at his hands. His weapons were gone. He then saw them at a nearby table. The ScizzorMen snickered.

"I'm going to tell Shorty he's awake," ScizzorMan C declared. He exited the room. ScizzorMan A smiled.

"Welcome to PS 244," he announced. "I hope you enjoy your stay."

Paperboy was puzzled for a moment. Then he remembered. This was Scott's school! This was the school that was taken over by LOEP!

" Why did you bring me here?" Paperboy asked.

"To fight," ScizzorMan A answered.

Paperboy did not understand. Suddenly, Shorty Scarface entered the room.

"Hello, Michael," he said in an evil tone. Paperboy didn't answer. "You're probably wondering where you are and why you are here. You're at LOEP's second base, PS 244. You are here to fight in a tournament."

"I'm not interested," Paperboy said flatly.

"I didn't give you a choice. Besides, I have a nice proposal for you. If you enter and win this tournament, LOEP will not take over PS 266. Nobody from LOEP will ever come there again. Interested now?"

"Maybe," Paperboy responded.

" When we took over the school," Shorty continued, "We made the students our prisoners. They were prisoners of their own school. If you lose, Paperboy, you too must become a prisoner of PS 244 ."

Paperboy didn't know what to do. Scott told him about his experience as a prisoner of PS 244. But this was a chance for Paperboy to save his school. Paperboy decided to take a chance.

"I accept your offer."

Shorty smiled. "You will face your first opponent later. If you win, you enter the semifinals. If you win the semifinals, you enter the finals. Once you've won the finals, you have won the tournament." Shorty turned to leave. "Someone will escort you to the arena when it is your turn to fight."

" Where is James?" Paperboy demanded.

"He's in another room being told about the tournament. He's entering it too. Won't it be interesting if you have to fight him to save your school." Shorty chuckled. "By the way, a girl came here to save you and your friend. She was a very good fighter. So she's going to enter the tournament as well. Her name is Nina."

Paperboy couldn't believe it. Nina must have followed the ScizzorMen here. Paperboy had to find a way for James and Nina to escape. He had to fight this tournament. Not his friends.

"When does the tournament start?" Paperboy asked.

"You'll know when it starts," Shorty answered. "You're in the first match." Shorty exited the room and ScizzorMan A and B followed him.

"Do you really want to do this?" ScizzorMan A asked Shorty. "It's very risky."

"Jason's entering the tournament," Shorty said flatly.

"Jason?" ScizzorMan A was confused.

"You don't know Jason?" ScizzorMan B asked in surprise. "Some people call him Copycat. He's never lost a tournament." ScizzorMan B smiled and looked toward his brother. "Start making room. We're going to have a new prisoner soon."

14

THREE

Paperboy was nervous. This was the riskiest thing he had ever done. If he won, LOEP would not take over his school. All the bullies at PS 266 would leave and never come back. But if he lost, he would become a prisoner of PS 244. The thought of being a prisoner of LOEP was terrifying. It was also terrifying to know he might have to fight James or Nina to save his school. Paperboy sighed. He wondered if he should have accepted Shorty's conditions. He also wondered about his brother. Didn't Scott see him fight the Scizzormen at PS 266? Paperboy wondered what Scott would do after that. Suddenly the door opened. Scissorman C was at the door.

"Come with me," he ordered. Paperboy went to the table and grabbed his weapons. He put his paper airplanes, PBB's, and paper claws in their proper positions on his hands and put his paper lasers in his pockets. He then followed Scissorman C. Scissorman C led him out of his room and to two giant doors.

"You will now face your first opponent," Scizzorman C announced. "Are you ready?"

"Yes," Paperboy answered.

Scizzorman C smiled. "Go through the doors then."

Paperboy went through the doors and found himself in a playground. There were bullies all around him; and there was a path Paperboy followed to the middle of the playground. He found himself standing next to a large boy. Another boy was on the opposite side of the large boy. Paperboy guessed this was the person he was going to fight.

" On my right, we have Paperboy!" The large boy shouted at the top of his lungs. All the bullies booed. "On my left we have John!" All the bullies cheered. John smiled a little.

"Ready?" The large boy shouted. Suddenly some of the bullies stood on the path Paperboy had followed, closing it off to Paperboy and John. This formed a complete circle of bullies around Paperboy. "Fight!" The large boy shouted. He then moved into the crowd.

Suddenly John ran to Paperboy and punched him. Paperboy fell from surprise. John then jumped on him. Paperboy groaned and pushed John off of him. He then got up.

"I don't want to do this," Paperboy announced. "Just surrender."

"Never!" John exclaimed.

John tried to kick Paperboy. Paperboy dodged the attack and attacked John with his paper airplanes.

"OHHHHH," John cried out in pain.

Paperboy tripped John. John landed on the ground with a thud. He struggled to get back up.

"No," John whispered. "I can't lose."

Once John was on his feet, he shouted at Paperboy, "I can't lose!"

Paperboy was surprised by this outburst. Taking advantage of the moment, John punched Paperboy mercilessly.

"I can't lose! I must be free!"

Paperboy fell to the ground. He looked at John. John was crying.

"What?" Paperboy asked.

"If I win this tournament, I'll become a member of LOEP. I won't be a prisoner of PS 244 anymore!

"Do you really want to join LOEP?" Paperboy asked.

"No," John replied. "But I'll do anything to escape this school."

Paperboy was shocked. John wasn't fighting just to fight. Like him, he was fighting for a reason.

"I must win this tournament," John said. "I have to!"

" I'm sorry," Paperboy said tears in his eyes. " But I have to win. I can't afford to lose."

"Neither can I!" John exclaimed.

John prepared to jump on Paperboy again. But before he could jump, Paperboy got up and attacked him with his paper airplanes. John fell. But before he hit the ground, Paperboy grabbed him with his paper claw and threw him 5 feet away from him. John landed on the ground with a loud thud. Paperboy could see this was all John could take. But John's will would not let him give up. Paperboy watched as John slowly stood up.

"I must win. I can't go back. I'll die there."

Now Paperboy was crying.

"I'm sorry," he repeated.

Paperboy unwillingly threw a PBB at John.

"OHHHHHHH," John cried out in pain. This was more than John could handle. He fell to the ground. Paperboy know he would not get back up. As much as John wanted to win, his body could not handle any more paper cuts.

"No," John whispered.

The crowd waited one minute. Then they started counting down in unison.

"Ten, nine, eight, seven, six, five, four, three, two, one, finished!"

Paperboy watched as John was carried away by bullies.

"No! I can still fight. Don't take me back. Please, noooooo!"

Paperboy was still crying as the bullies carried John away. The crowd then disappeared inside the building. Suddenly Shorty Scarface was in front of Paperboy.

"Very good," Shorty commended. "Two more to go."

Paperboy froze. He had to do this two more times? He had to crush someone's hopes of escaping PS 244 two more times? Paperboy slowly walked inside the building. Inside, he saw a short kid with a mask on his face. This kid reminded Paperboy of someone he could not possibly be. Paperboy saw James and Nina. He quickly ran over to them.

"Hi," Paperboy said. James and Nina turned to face him.

"You're all right!" James exclaimed.

"Where have you been?" Nina asked.

"I just finished the first round." Paperboy said sadly.

"Is something wrong?" James asked.

"I can't do this," Paperboy admitted. "I just fought this boy who only entered the tournament because he was told he would no longer be a prisoner of this school if he won. He would become a member of LOEP."

"That's not..."

"He didn't even want to become part of LOEP!" Paperboy

interrupted. "He just didn't want to remain a prisoner of PS 244." Paperboy started crying again. "I defeated him. I crushed his dreams, just to achieve mine." James and Nina looked at each other, then at Paperboy.

"What did Shorty Scarface tell you?" Nina asked.

"If I win, LOEP will not take over PS 266. If I lose, I become a prisoner of PS 244," Paperboy answered.

"He told me and James if we win, we escape this school with you. But if we lose, we will never see you again."

"We have to escape," James announced. "What if we have to fight each other?"

" *You* have to escape," Paperboy answered. "I have to save my school," he sighed. "No matter what it takes." Nina looked away from Paperboy.

"You see that kid with the mask?" Nina asked. Paperboy and James looked at the kid.

"He's been looking at me since he got here. I don't like it."

"He reminds me of someone."

"Who?" James and Nina said in unison.

"He reminds me of."

"Nina!" Shorty interrupted. "You're next."

Nina looked at Shorty. She deliberately pushed him to the side and exited into the playground.

Shorty opened the door and prepared to step out.

"Don't try anything, Max," Paperboy said. "You're only going to hurt yourself."

Shorty turned and walked toward Paperboy. "When you lose this tournament," he said, you're going to wish you never said that." He then walked away from Paperboy; deeper into the building.

Paperboy noticed the kid in the mask was gone. A pencil lay where he was standing. Suddenly fear took over Paperboy. He went to the pencil and picked it up. *It is him*," Paperboy thought.

Meanwhile, Shorty Scarface went up to what used to be the principal's office. He found Jason engaged in a thumb war with Scizzorman B.

"Jason," Shorty called. Jason stopped and looked at Shorty Scarface. "Paperboy's getting me angry. If you face him, show him no mercy."

"No problem," Jason answered in Shorty's voice. " But first I have to fight a boy named James to get into the semifinals. Should I go easy on him?"

"Just a little bit," Shorty answered. He smiled and looked out the window. "Michael has no idea what he's up against."

FOUR

Paperboy and James waited anxiously for Nina to come out. She could not lose this tournament. None of them could afford to lose. Unfortunately, there could only be one winner. Suddenly, the doors opened. The kid with the mask came out, drenched and battered.

"Oh no," James uttered.

Nina must not have won. Bullies started coming through the doors. The match was over. Nina did not win. Both Paperboy and James realized this.

"Where is she?" James asked worriedly. "I've got to find her." James started to skate out the door.

"James!" Shorty shouted. James turned around to face Shorty Scarface. "You're next," Shorty declared.

"Where is Nina?" James demanded.

"Nina's dead," Shorty announced. "Or at least she should be. But knowing her, she's probably resisting her fate."

"You can't do that!" James screamed. "You said if she lost she will never see Paperboy again.

"I kept my promise," Shorty said defensively. "She never will see Paperboy again. Because she's going to die."

"No!" James shouted. "You're going to pay -"

"You can't do that," Paperboy announced. Shorty turned to Paperboy.

"Why not?" he asked.

"We made a deal," Paperboy recalled. "If I win, my school is safe from you. This includes everyone from my school. You can't."

"No," Shorty interrupted. "If you win, LOEP will not take over your school and all the bullies would leave. That was not part of the deal."

"Fine," Paperboy uttered. "Let's make it a part of the deal. If I win, LOEP will not take over my school. All the bullies will leave PS 266. And they can never bother anyone from PS 266 again. If I lose, I become a prisoner PS 244. Deal?" Shorty thought about it.

"Deal," he agreed. "I'll tell the bullies that are with Nina." Shorty smiled. "I just hope I'm not too late. And either way, you're never going to see her again." Shorty then walked away. Paperboy sighed. He hoped his new deal was not constructed too late. James sighed.

"I'm next," He announced.

"Good luck," Paperboy said. James looked at Paperboy. He then went through the doors. Suddenly a light skinned boy with nappy hair approached Paperboy.

"So you're Paperboy," the boy said. "I heard a lot about you. I'm Jason." Jason extended his hand.

"Are you fighting James?" Paperboy asked.

"Yes," Jason answered.

"Why are you in the tournament?" Paperboy asked.

"To copy more and more people," he answered. Paperboy was puzzled. "If I ever face you," Jason said smiling, "you'd understand what I meant." He then went through the doors. Paperboy sat down on the floor. He remembered John. Paperboy thought about John for 10 minutes. Suddenly the doors opened. Jason stepped out. He walked over to Paperboy.

"Your friend has some nice tricks," he commented. "But they're not just his tricks anymore." Jason walked away. Paperboy couldn't believe it. James lost too. At least he was safe.

"Michael!" Shorty shouted. "You're next."

Paperboy went to Shorty. "Is Nina alive?" he asked.

"Yes," Shorty replied. "You're lucky. Very lucky." Shorty then went through the doors. Paperboy sighed. He did not know if he was ready to crush someone's dreams again. With PS 266 in mind, Paperboy walked through the doors. Once outside, he followed the path to the large boy and stood beside him. Paperboy looked on the large boy's opposite side. He could not believe his eyes. It was the kid in the mask!

"On my right hand side, we have Paperboy!" the large boy shouted. All the bullies booed. "On my left hand side, we have the Mad Hunter!" All the bullies cheered. Paperboy was afraid of this. The kid in the mask was the Mad Hunter. But how could that be possible?

"Fight!" The large boy shouted.

"Billy?" Paperboy asked. "Is that you?"

"No," The Mad Hunter replied. "It's me. But you wouldn't recognize me, even if I took my mask off."

"But how?" Paperboy asked. "How did you survive that trap?"

"I didn't," The Mad Hunter replied. "I was ruined. My hands, my feet, my legs, but....... my face. My face is the worst of all. It's not..... normal. It's not human. But that's OK. Because I'm not human. I'm a hunter. I am the Mad Hunter!"

The Mad Hunter tackled Paperboy to the ground. He stood up and took out a ruler with a rope tied on it (a bow) and a pencil (an arrow). He fired the pencil. Paperboy dodged the pencil and quickly got back on his feet. He then attacked the Mad Hunter with his paper airplanes.

"AHHHHH!" the Mad Hunter cried out in pain. Paperboy tripped the Mad Hunter. Before he fell, Paperboy grabbed him with his paper claw (which pierced the Mad Hunter) and swung him as far as he could. Paperboy took out his paper laser. The Mad Hunter hit the ground. Paperboy prepared to fire. Then he stopped.

"Why are you in this tournament?" Paperboy asked.

"To slay my prey," The Mad Hunter answered. "They would not let me destroy her. But I will destroy my prey. I will destroy her for what she's done. She turned my face into the face of a monster. But this," the Mad Hunter said pointing to his mask, " is the face of a hunter."

The Mad Hunter got up and charged at Paperboy. Paperboy fired his paper laser. The Mad Hunter dodged the paper balls and punched Paperboy with all his strength. Paperboy fell five feet back from the Mad Hunter. The attack was so powerful Paperboy dropped his paper laser. The Mad Hunter then fired pencils from his ruler. Paperboy was too weak to dodge the pencils. Each pencil hit him. The Mad Hunter walked over to a greatly weakened Paperboy like a spider walks to a trapped fly. He looked down at his former prey. He then put a pencil on the rope, pulled back, and aimed at Paperboy. Suddenly the crowd started to count down.

"Ten, nine, eight, seven, six, five, four, three, two-"

"NOOOOO!" Paperboy screamed.

Paperboy stood up. The Mad Hunter fired the pencil. The pencil hit Paperboy and he fell back down. The Mad Hunter took out another pencil, put it on the rope, aimed, and pulled back.

"Ten, nine, eight, seven, six, five-"

Paperboy quickly threw a PBB at the Mad Hunter.

"AHHHHH!" The Mad Hunter cried out in pain. Paperboy took advantage of the moment and stood up. He then attacked the Mad Hunter with his paper airplanes. Before the Mad Hunter could react to this attack, Paperboy grabbed him with his paper claw and threw him five feet into the air. Once the Mad Hunter was within an arm's reach, Paperboy grabbed him with his paper claw and slammed him to the ground.

"Never attack any of my friends again," he ordered.

"OHHHHHH," the Mad Hunter groaned. The crowd waited one minute. Then they counted down.

"Ten, nine, eight, seven, six, five, four, three, two, one, finished!" The large boy moved out of the crowd.

"Paperboy is the winner!"

The bullies cleared a path for Paperboy to walk through the doors. Once inside, Paperboy stumbled and then sat down on the floor. He was greatly weakened. He had no more PBB's and only one paper laser.

"That was for Nina," Paperboy thought.

Meanwhile, Jason looked out the window of what used to be the principal's office. He had seen the entire fight.

"Paperboy is quite an opponent," he said to himself.

"But he has one weakness. He cares too much for his friends." Jason chuckled. "That will be his downfall," he said in James' voice.

Chapter 5
The Ultimate Opposition

FIVE

Paperboy was out of luck. He did not have many weapons left for the final match of the tournament and he was not at full strength. He had no idea where James and Nina were, or if he'd ever see them again. But he had to overcome the odds. He could not lose the final match. Suddenly, Jason walked up to Paperboy.

"I'll see you in the final match," he said slyly. Jason then walked through the doors.

Paperboy was confused. *"How did Jason know he was in the finals?"*

Meanwhile, Scott arrived at the doors of PS 244. He was here for one reason: to save James and Nina. He had seen James and a masked character fighting the Scizzormen. Scott regretted not helping them. They were defeated in battle and abducted by the Scizzormen. Shortly after the incident, Nina tried to rescue them. Scott knew she was captured too. One person cannot defeat the Scizzormen.

"Well," Scott thought, *"with one exception."*

Scott also knew where the Scizzormen had taken James, Nina, and the masked figure. He knew this because this was not the first time he'd seen someone captured by LOEP. James and Nina were at his old school, PS 244. They were probably being forced to become prisoners of the school. Scott devised a plan to save them. However, he was not sure about the masked figure. Who was he? And why was he fighting the Scizzormen? Why was James fighting the Scizzormen? Scott put these questions aside. They would be answered later. He opened the door. Inside, 10 bullies stood at each end of the hallway. Once they saw Scott, they took out their scissor guns and aimed. One bully walked up to Scott.

"What do you want?" he asked.

"I want James and Nina." Scott replied. The bully looked confused. "The Scizzormen captured them today," Scott recalled.

"Oh yes," the bully remembered. "Sorry. They are in a tournament right now." The bully studied Scott. " Are you a member?" he asked.

"No," Scott replied. The bully's face turned into a mix of curiosity and strictness. But before he could say another word, Scott punched him to the ground. The remaining bullies looked at the bully on the floor, then at Scott. They fired their scissor guns. Ploc! Ploc! Ploc! Scott dodged every single scissor. He then punched a bully, took his scissor gun, and tripped him. He grabbed another bully, and threw him into eight other bullies. All the bullies fell to the ground. He then fired his scissor gun at another bully. The bully fell to the ground. Scott picked up his scissor gun, grabbed another bully, and threw him into the remaining bullies. Scott picked up another scissor gun and ran into PS 244, untouched.

Meanwhile, Paperboy watched as Jason came through the doors. Jason walked past Paperboy and then further into the building. Ten minutes later, Shorty Scarface walked up to Paperboy.

"It is time for the final round. Go through the doors and face your fate."

Paperboy looked at Shorty. He then went through the doors. Outside, Paperboy followed the path to the large boy. He then looked to the side of the large boy. Paperboy was not surprised by who he saw. It was Jason.

"On my right hand side, we have Paperboy!" The large boy howled. All the bullies booed. "On my left hand side, we have the tournament champion, Copycat!"

The crowd was in an uproar. They chanted "Copycat! Copycat! Copycat! Copycat!" One minute later, they quieted down.

"Fight!" The large boy ordered. He then moved into the crowd. Paperboy looked at Jason. He noticed he had a knapsack on his back.

"How did you know you would be in the finals?" he asked.

"I'm always in the finals," Jason answered. "And I always win. I've never lost in a tournament."

" How many tournaments have you competed in?" Paperboy asked.

"Twenty five," Jason answered.

This surprised Paperboy. Jason suddenly dashed to Paperboy and punched him. He then tripped him. Suddenly Jason ran out of the playground and back into the building. That is when Paperboy noticed the bullies never closed the path to the building this time. Paperboy decided to wait for Jason. Suddenly, after five minutes, James skated through the door and to Paperboy. Paperboy was surprised to see James.

"Paperboy!" James exclaimed. "It's good to see you. I found a way to escape. Let's go!"

"No," Paperboy answered. "I already told you I have to win the tournament. I'm in the final round! By the way, where is Nina?"

"Nina is waiting for us," James said. "There'll always be time to save your school. We need to leave now. I won't go without you. Or at least help us make it out safely."

"OK," Paperboy agreed. "But just so you can make it out. Then I'm going back to finish the tournament."

Paperboy started running to the door. Suddenly two protractors pierced his feet. Ropes then came out of the protractors and bounded Paperboy's body tightly, making him immobile. Paperboy fell.

"James!" Paperboy called. "Help!"

James walked over to Paperboy. He smiled. "You're so predictable. You still think I'm your friend. Surprise! It's me. Copycat."

"Jason?" Paperboy asked. "But you look like James. You sound like James."

"Yes. Do you know why I ran away? I ran away to change. Inside my knapsack lies all the masks and accessories I need to look like anyone I want. And the voice mimicking is my very special talent. You better get up soon. Because if you don't, I win."

Paperboy couldn't believe it. Jason made himself look like James! He even sounded like James. And now Paperboy was caught in a protractor trap! He had to get out and stand up before the crowd started counting down. Suddenly Paperboy had an idea. Paperboy rolled to Copycat. Copycat tripped. Paperboy then rolled over one of Copycat's protractors. The protractor cut the ropes. Paperboy then stood up and took the protractors out of his foot. Copycat then stood up. He skated to Paperboy and attacked him with his protractors. Paperboy fell to the ground, and realized something.

He couldn't do this. Even though it was not James, Copycat looked just like him. And Paperboy could not attack his friend. Paperboy stood up. Copycat attacked with his protractors. Paperboy dodged the attack. Copycat tripped Paperboy. Paperboy fell to the ground. Copycat then attacked with his protractors. Paperboy dodged the attack and realized something. This was not James. This was Jason, and Jason was determined to win the tournament. Paperboy could not let that happen. He had to fight back. Paperboy stood up and attacked Copycat with his paper airplanes.

"AHHHHHH!" he cried out in pain. Paperboy stumbled. He sounded just like James. Copycat took advantage of the moment and attacked Paperboy mercilessly with his protractors. Paperboy fell to the ground. Suddenly Copycat picked Paperboy up and threw him up in the air. Once Paperboy was in arm's reach, Copycat grabbed him and slammed him to the ground. The attack was so powerful Paperboy dropped one of his paper airplanes. Copycat waited to see if Paperboy would stand up. Paperboy slowly stood up, his will pushing him to win.

"For PS 266," he said.

With that Paperboy attacked Copycat fiercely with his paper airplanes. Copycat fell to the ground. Paperboy picked Copycat up with his paper claw and threw him up in the air. He then took out his paper lasers and fired at Copycat while he was in the air. When Copycat was in arm's reach, Paperboy grabbed him with his paper claw and punched him with all his strength. Copycat fell back seven feet. The attack was so powerful Copycat dropped one of his protractors.

Meanwhile, Scott had gotten very close to the playground. He defeated many bullies, and none managed to touch him. Scott turned the corner. He then saw one of the Scizzormen. His back was to Scott. Scott smiled. This will be easy. Scott crept up in back of the Scizzorman. Once he was in arm's reach, he grabbed the Scizzorman's feet, and swung him to a nearby wall. He punched the Scizzorman and took his scissor gun. He fired the scissor gun. Ploc! Ploc! All the scissors hit the Scizzorman.

"OHHHHH," the Scizzorman groaned.

Suddenly Scizzorman B and C walked down the hallway. They spotted Scott.

"What are you doing here?" They asked in unison. Scott ran back around the corner and waited. Scizzorman B and C turned the corner. There was nobody there. Suddenly Scott jumped out from behind Scizzormen B and punched him to the ground. He then picked him up and punched him five times. He took Scizzorman B's scissor gun and threw him into Scizzorman C. Scott ran down the hallway. The two Scizzormen groaned and stood up. But they were too late. Scott was gone.

"Spread the word." Scizzorman B said. "We are under attack. Scott's in the building."

Scizzorman C ran to do what Scizzorman B told him to do. Scizzorman B then walked to his ambushed brother.

Meanwhile, the fight between Paperboy and Copycat raged on.

They had been fighting for half an hour now and both fighters were getting tired. Copycat tried to attack with his protractor, but he missed. Paperboy then fired his paper laser. Copycat deflected the paper balls and knocked the paper laser out of Paperboy's hand. He then attacked with his protractors. Paperboy tried to attack with his paper airplane, but he missed. He then tripped Copycat. Copycat landed with a thud. Paperboy stumbled. He had barely any strength left. Any minute now he could fall and would not be able to get up. Copycat was in the same condition.

Copycat secretly set up a protractor trap. He then stood up. Paperboy had to end this fight. Paperboy decided to make a desperate attempt. Paperboy charged at Copycat. Using every ounce of his remaining strength, Paperboy tackled him. They both fell right in the middle of the protractor trap. Paperboy fell beside Copycat as the protractors dashed to them. One protractor pierced Copycat's foot and another pierced Paperboy's. Ropes then came out of the protractors and bound both Paperboy and Copycat. Neither fighter was strong enough to try to release themselves. After a minute, the crowd started counting down.

"Ten, nine, eight, seven, six, five, four, three, two, one,.... finished?" They wondered. The large boy moved out of the crowd.

"This has never happened before.... I guess it's a tie."

"NOOOOO!" Shorty screamed. He moved out of the crowd.

"Paperboy was supposed to lose! This can't be possible!"

"What should we do now?" the large boy asked Shorty. Shorty thought about it. Then he came up with an evil idea.

"There is no winner," he announced. "It's a draw," he walked over to Paperboy.

"Too bad we didn't make a deal if there was a tie. I'll just have to come up with my own deal. Nina and James become prisoners of PS 244. Deal?" Michael groaned.

"Deal," Shorty answered himself.

"What about Paperboy?"

"Destroy him," Shorty ordered.

Suddenly the large boy was struck by a scissor. He then fell. Everyone watched as Scott walked past Shorty Scarface. Shorty grew angry. Scott walked toward Paperboy.

"Who are you?" he asked in curiosity. Scott removed Paperboy's mask. He then gasped.

"Michael?" Scott asked.

"Scott," Michael uttered. "Help."

Then, in front of Copycat, Shorty Scarface, and the crowd of bullies ready to destroy him and Scott, Michael fainted from fatigue.

SIX

"Are you sure it was just a fall?"

"I was there when it happened."

"That must have been quite a fall."

"OHHHH," Michael groaned. He turned on his side and slowly opened his eyes. The first person he saw was Mr. Raptor. Michael was suddenly alert. He found himself in a bed in a room with Mr. Raptor, his father.

"Are you OK?" Mr. Raptor asked.

"I will be," Michael answered. Michael then remembered his weapons. He looked at his hands. His weapons were gone.

"I heard you had quite a fall," Mr. Raptor recalled. Michael remembered tackling Copycat and trapping Copycat and himself in a protractor trap.

"Yeah," Michael answered. "Quite a fall," Michael then noticed Scott behind Mr. Raptor.

"I'll get you some water," Mr. Raptor announced. He then exited the room, leaving Michael and Scott. Michael turned to Scott.

"Where am I?" He asked.

"My room," Scott answered.

"How did I get here?" Michael asked. "The last thing I remember is Shorty Scarface ordering the bullies to destroy me, then you came and....... and that's all I remember."

"Shorty ordered the bullies to destroy me and you," Scott recalled.

"I fought off the bullies and escaped PS 244 with you."

"But how?" Michael asked. "There were at least 40 bullies out there. How did you get me out of the protractor trap?"

"Scissors," Scott replied. "As for the bullies, they were easy to defeat. Bullies are not smart, and they all think alike. If you can defeat one bully, you can defeat one hundred bullies. Now you answer a question for me. Why were you fighting the Scizzormen? And why were you in a paper mask and cape?"

"Well," Michael started, "like you, I also have a problem with LOEP. LOEP is trying to take over my school. I decided to try to stop them by becoming Paperboy. I have given bullies painful paper cuts and I've been defending my school from LOEP. James and Nina have helped me and are still helping me in trying to destroy LOEP."

"I understand now," Scott said. " But why did you enter the tournament?"

"Shorty told me if I win the tournament, my school will never be bothered again by LOEP."

"So you entered to save PS 266. Now I understand."

Mr. Raptor walked through the door and handed Michael a glass of water.

"I'll leave you two alone," Mr. Raptor said closing the door. Michael drank his water.

"I like these paper airplanes," Scott said with admiration. "It's a very good weapon."

"Thanks," Michael answered. Michael drank the rest of his water and asked Scott the question that was troubling him the most.

"What are we going to do about James and Nina?" Scott's face became strict.

"We're going to rescue them. The problem is Max knows we will come back for them. He will probably set up a trap."

"We'll have to take a chance," Michael stated.

"We have to come up with a plan," Scott agreed. "James and Nina have become prisoners of PS 244. This means they must be in...... the basement." Scott shivered a little. He hated that place. "All the prisoners are kept in the basement. James and Nina must be there too, under heavy guard. We have to get in the basement, rescue them, and leave before Max finds out we were there. There are bullies at the entrance doors to the basement, and in the basement. There might also be bullies in the hallways. We have to defeat them. The bullies in the basement usually have the keys to free the prisoners. I'll fight the bullies. You take their keys and free James and Nina. Then we'll get out of the basement and out of PS 244 before Max knows what happened."

"It sounds perfect," Michael said, pleased with his brother's plan.

"Just one thing," Scott said seriously. " Don't get separated from me or let me get separated from you. We can't save James and Nina if we don't know if one another is safe. This plan will fail if we are separated."

"I understand," Michael answered.

"We're also going to need weapons." Scott looked at Michael.

"You have paper?" Michael asked.

"I have a ton of paper."

Michael smiled. "Then let's prepare to save James and Nina."

Michael spent two hours creating paper airplanes, PBB's, paper claws, and paper lasers. He then showed Scott how to use these weapons. Scott showed Michael stealth techniques they would use in PS 244. The two brothers later talked about many different things. They shared jokes and secrets. That night Michael and Scott became more than just brothers. They became best friends.

Meanwhile, Shorty thought of a way to deal with the future arrival of Michael and Scott. Copycat was resting and the Scizzormen were guarding James and Nina. Shorty knew Michael and Scott would come back for their friends. He had to come up with an idea. Suddenly an idea struck Shorty. *Most likely Michael and Scott would try to save their friends. What would happen if they got separated, only to meet up with someone who looked like (but was not) their missing partner?* Shorty then went to Jason's room to discuss this plan of chaos.

Michael then prepared to go to sleep. He was still tired from the tournament. Scott said he would sleep on the couch downstairs. Michael had a long day today. He was abducted by the Scizzormen, completed an entire tournament, and planned a rescue attempt all in one day! Michael sighed. Tomorrow would hold more obstacles for Michael to overcome. With that, Michael fell asleep, with no idea of what Shorty Scarface had planned for him and Scott.

SEVEN

Michael tossed and turned in his sleep. "No." He whispered. "I'm sorry." No. Nooooo!'"

Michael's eyes popped open and he sat up. He could not believe it. He had had a bad nightmare about John as a prisoner of PS 244. Even though the tournament was finished, the effects of it still lingered in Michael. Michael was worried about John. *What were they doing to him? What could they have done to him so he would enter a tournament to win his freedom, just to join an organization he did not want to be part of?* Michael shivered at the possible answers.

Michael laid in bed. He was afraid to go back to sleep. However, twenty minutes later, sleep conquered him. Unfortunately, later on that night Michael had the same nightmare again.

"Nooooo!" Michael uttered. His eyes popped open once more, but again sleep overcame him. Michael awoke after a restless night, as sunlight splashed on him. The door opened. Scott stepped in the room.

"Good morning," he said cheerfully.

"Good morning," Michael said flatly.

"Did you sleep well?"

Michael shook his head. "Nightmares," he replied.

"I'm sorry to hear that, but either way we have to start getting ready. I told dad where Paperboy might be today. That way he won't know we were gone."

"Where did you tell him Paperboy might be?"

"In the corner of PS 266's playground," Scott smiled. "He already left the house for school."

"Perfect," Michael replied.

Michael started to get ready to go to PS 244. Scott went downstairs to prepare to leave, too. Michael got up from the bed, stretched, took a shower, got dressed, made breakfast, ate breakfast, and then changed into his Paperboy costume. Paperboy armed himself with weapons. He put two paper airplanes (one on each hand) between his pointer and middle finger; four PBB's (two on each hand) between his middle, index, and pinky fingers; four paper lasers (one in each pocket) in his two front pockets and two back pockets;, and two paper claws (one on each hand) on both of his hands. Paperboy then went to his brother. Scott had the same amount of weapons Paperboy had, and in the same places. The only thing Scott did not have was a mask and cape.

"Ready?" Scott asked.

"Let's go," Paperboy replied.

Paperboy and Scott left the house and walked to PS 244. Once there, they both looked at each other to see if the other was ready. They both nodded and entered PS 244. Inside, ten bullies stood on each side of the hallway. They all looked at Paperboy and Scott.

"They're here!" a bully shouted. Suddenly all the bullies started running away. Scott thought about their action for a moment and was alarmed.

"Stop them!" Scott ordered. "Don't let any of them get away!"

Paperboy ran to a fleeing bully and tripped him. Scott tripped another bully and took his scissor gun. He fired at two bullies.

Paperboy took out his paper laser and fired at the floor ahead of him. Three bullies tripped on the paper balls. Paperboy and Scott ran to the remaining bullies. Scott threw the scissor gun at one bully, hitting him on his head. The bully fell. The remaining bullies split up and fled into separate hallways.

"We can't catch them all now", Scott uttered. "This is not good. Usually they would stay and fight. Soon Max will know we are here. We have to work fast."

Paperboy and Scott followed their plan to rescue James and Nina. Every corner Scott turned Paperboy looked behind him as Scott looked down the hallway. They then moved together down the hallway, as quiet as they could be. After five minutes Scott said, "We are close to the basement. Remember, stay close."

They didn't see the four bullies creeping up on them from the back. Two bullies grabbed Scott and attacked him. Scott then fell to the floor in surprise. Before Paperboy could react to this, the remaining bullies grabbed him and covered his eyes. Scott got up and attacked the bullies with his paper airplanes. The bullies fell to the floor. They then saw somebody approaching Scott. The bullies reluctantly got back up. Scott watched the bullies get up as the person behind him raised his fist. Before Scott could attack the two bullies, the person behind him struck. Scott was knocked out by the blow. He fell to the ground. The bullies grabbed him and carried him away.

Paperboy pierced the bully's hand that was covering his eyes. The bully fell to the floor. He then attacked the other bully with his paper airplane. Paperboy saw Scott in front of him. He was glad to see his brother was okay.

"We have to be more careful," Paperboy announced.

"Yeah." Scott smiled, "More careful."

Paperboy and Scott walked down the rest of the hallway.

"I know a different way to get to James and Nina," Scott said. Paperboy looked at him.

"Let's stick to the plan," Paperboy replied.

"Lead the way."

Scott smiled. "Sure," he answered. Scott led Paperboy far away from the basement and to two giant doors. Paperboy suddenly stopped. He went through those doors during the tournament.

"This is the way to the basement?" Paperboy asked.

"Yes," Scott replied. Scott led him through the doors and outside, to the playground.

"Here we are," Scott announced.

"This isn't the basement!" Paperboy shouted. He then looked at Scott and noticed something was wrong.

"Where are your paper weapons?" he asked. Scott smiled.

"It's me again, Paperboy."

Paperboy was confused for a moment. Then he shivered.

"Copycat?"

Copycat smiled and tackled Paperboy to the ground. Paperboy pushed Copycat off him and stood up. Copycat got up and approached Paperboy. Paperboy fired a PBB at Copycat.

"Ahhhhhhh!" Copycat cried out in pain.

Paperboy attacked Copycat fiercely with his paper airplanes.

"How could you do this?" Paperboy shouted angrily. "Where is Scott?"

Copycat smiled and replied, "New weapons."

Paperboy was confused.

"What else is new?" Copycat asked.

Paperboy ignored Copycat and attacked with his paper airplanes. Copycat dodged the attack and tripped Paperboy. His face grew serious.

"You know, I never had a draw in a tournament. You broke my winning streak. Now you are going to pay for that. Get him!"

Suddenly fifty bullies came through the doors and formed a circle around Paperboy. Copycat picked up the PBB Paperboy threw at him. He then turned to leave.

"Pay back time," Copycat said in an evil voice. He then left Paperboy with the bullies.

"How can I defeat all these bullies," Paperboy thought. Suddenly an idea struck him. *"All bullies think alike,"* he recalled.

Before any bully attacked Paperboy, he threw a PBB at a bully. The bully fell to the ground. Paperboy grabbed him and swung him into nine bullies. Paperboy then took out and fired his paper laser at a bully. The bully flinched. Paperboy grabbed the bully and threw him up into the air.

"Come on," he taunted the bullies.

The circle of bullies closed in on Paperboy. However, before any of them could attack Paperboy, the bully in the air came down and hit five other bullies who fell. Because the bullies were so close, the bullies that fell hit other bullies, who then fell, hit other bullies, who then fell, and so on. Paperboy watched as the domino effect knocked bully after bully to the ground. After one minute all the bullies were on the ground.

"They really aren't smart," Paperboy said in a sad tone.

Paperboy ran back to the doors. He then suddenly realized something frightening. The rescue plan had failed. The plan's only weakness had been discovered and exploited. The plan's weakness seemed so small, so easy to pass detection. But the weakness had been found and the worse thing that could possibly happen had taken place! Paperboy was separated from Scott.

CHAPTER 8
THE INVINCIBLE GUARDS

EIGHT

"Ohhhhhhhh," Scott groaned. His eyes slowly opened. The first person Scott saw was Shorty Scarface. Scott then saw Jason. Scott looked at his surroundings. He was lying on the floor in a small bare room with one table in the room. Scott looked at his hands. He still had all his paper weapons.

"This is good," Shorty said as he examined a scissor Jason handed him.

"This is what I need."

Scott had to get out of here. He had to find his brother and rescue James and Nina. He wondered if Michael was okay. Shorty turned to face Scott. His eyes lit up at the sight of seeing Scott awake.

"Leave, Jason!" Shorty ordered. "It is time." Jason left as Shorty had commanded. Shorty then walked over to Scott. Scott looked at Shorty.

"Where am I?" he asked.

"You're in one of PS 244's many storage rooms. Except," Shorty smiled, "I removed all that was stored." Shorty's smile grew bigger.

"It's over, Scott. The rescue is over. Michael is destroyed because of Jason. James and Nina are my prisoners. And best of all, you are at my mercy!"

"Michael's …….gone?" Scott asked in surprise. Shorty nodded his head.

"I'll never forgive you for this!" Scott exclaimed. " You're going to pay!"

Scott got up and charged at Shorty. Shorty quickly punched him. Scott fell back to the floor. Shorty looked down at Scott, the scissor in his hand.

"The reason you are here has nothing to do with Michael," Shorty announced. "You are here so I can return the favor!"

"You're still after me for that?" Scott asked

"You put a scar on my face!" Shorty shouted angrily. I will have this scar for the rest of my life. Even after you die, you will still haunt me. I can never forgive you, even if I wanted to! Because of "this," Shorty said pointing to the scar, "Now it is time for me to return the favor. You put a scar on my face, now I will put a scar on yours." Shorty held up the scissor and walked to Scott. Scott stood up.

"I wish James and Nina could see this," Shorty said, as he walked to Scott.

"I have their weapons," Shorty pointed to the table. On the table were protractors and water pens.

"What are you going to do after you return the favor?" Scott asked.

"I'm going to destroy you," Shorty replied. " Maybe I'll do it with those weapons," he said pointing back to the table.

"I'm sorry Max," Scott said flatly. "You're not going to put a scar on my face or destroy me."

"Really?" Shorty asked. "What's going to stop me?"

"Good question," Scott thought.

When Shorty was in arm's reach he reached out for Scott. Scott quickly ducked and rolled behind him. Shorty turned around.

"Don't make this hard, Scott," Shorty warned. "You'll pay for it sooner or later."

Scott anxiously wanted to fight Shorty Scarface. He wanted to get revenge for what LOEP had done to him and his brother. But he had to save James and Nina. He had to think of a way to escape. Suddenly Scott had an idea. He ran to the table with the protractor and water pens. He took the protractor. He had seen James use the protractors when he and Michael fought the Scizzormen at PS 266. Scott charged at Shorty. He attacked with the protractors. Shorty grabbed both of Scott's arms before he was hit with the protractors. He then violently swung Scott to a nearby wall. Scott hit the wall and bounced off hitting the floor with a thud..

Shorty walked to Scott.

Scott quickly executed his plan. "You know, Max, LOEP is the most pathetic organization in the world."

Shorty walked a little faster.

"You know why this organization is so pitiful? Because you are leading it. You know nothing about leadership. Look at your bullies. Their I.Q.'s can be compared to their attention span. They're both very, very low. But what do you expect when Max Parker is their leader?"

This was all Shorty could take. He ran to Scott and jumped in towards him. Scott quickly rolled away. He then watched as two protractors pierced Shorty's feet. Ropes then emerged from the protractors and bound Shorty, making him immobile. In surprise Shorty fell to the floor. Scott then quickly grabbed a protractor and water pen, opened the door and raced out as fast as he could.

"No!" Shorty shouted. Using only a small portion of his strength, he broke out of the protractor trap. He quickly took the protractors out of his feet and ran out the door to Scott. But he was too late. Scott was gone.

Meanwhile, Paperboy decided to retrace his steps. He went back to where Copycat had led him and found himself in the same hallway where he and Scott were ambushed.

"What should I do now?" Paperboy thought. He did not know how to get to the basement. Paperboy went to the end of the hallway. He looked around the corner. Reluctantly, Paperboy decided to try to find the basement. He just hoped he would not get lost. Suddenly, Paperboy heard footsteps behind him. He turned around. He saw Scott running towards him. Once Scott saw him he grinned and said,

"Michael! You're alive!" Scott ran to Paperboy and hugged him. "It's good to see you." But doubt quickly set in. Could this be Copycat? Paperboy pushed Scott off of him and raised his paper airplane to his face threateningly.

"Prove to me you're Scott," Paperboy ordered.

Scott understood what Paperboy was doing. He then recalled one of Michael's secrets.

"You tried to flush yourself down the toilet once when you were little because your mother told you that's where babies come from."

"Okay, it is you." Paperboy said, relieved. "I'm sorry about that. It's just because Jason's around …. I don't know who is who anymore."

"It's okay," Scott replied. "Right now we have a bigger problem. I just escaped from Max and he is not happy about it. It's good that you were here. I was going to the basement. We don't have any more time for stealth. We have to get James and Nina now."

Paperboy and Scott ran down two hallways. They turned a corner. At the end of this hallway was a door. Five bullies guarded the door.

Paperboy and Scott slowly crept up on the bullies. Once they were close enough, Scott threw a PBB at one bully. The bully fell to the floor. Before any of the other bullies could react, Scott dashed to a bully, grabbed him and threw him into the other bullies. All the bullies fell to the floor.

"Let's go," Scott whispered.

Paperboy ran to the door. Scott opened the door. Paperboy stepped through first. Inside, he found a stairway. At the end of the stairway he saw several doors. A bully guarded each door. Paperboy also heard screams. He thought about John. His thought was interrupted as Scott came down the steps.

"James and Nina are in one of those rooms," Scott whispered. The bully that is guarding the door has the key to only that door. I'll have to defeat all the bullies. You open the door and find James and Nina."

Suddenly, Paperboy spotted Scizzorman A walking past a bully's door. He talked to the bully. He then talked loud enough so that everyone could hear.

"Everyone, be on the lookout for Paperboy and Scott. Max has just informed me that Scott has escaped and Copycat's trap failed. Paperboy is not dead. They might come down here any minute now. If you need me I will be guarding James and Nina's room."

"We understand," the bullies replied in unison. Scizzorman A then walked away from the bully.

"Change of plans," Scott whispered." Keep your eye on Scizzorman A. Tell me when he stops by a door."

Paperboy watched Scizzorman A. Scizzorman A walked past 20 doors. He stopped at a door. Paperboy then noticed Scizzorman B and C were at that door also.

"He stopped," Paperboy informed Scott.

"I'll handle the bullies. You fight Scizzorman A, take the key and free James and Nina."

"It's not just Scizzorman A," Paperboy replied.

Scott ran to a bully and attacked him with his paper airplane. Paperboy ran to the Scizzormen. Once the Scizzormen saw him they shouted,

"Paperboy!"

Paperboy then attacked Scizzorman A with his paper airplanes.

"AHHHHHHHHH!" the Scizzorman cried out in pain.

Suddenly Scizzorman B tackled Paperboy to the ground. He then picked him up and held him. Scizzorman C took out his scizzor gun and aimed. Before he could fire, Paperboy pierced Scizzorman B's hand with his paper claw. He then fired a PBB at Scizzorman C. Before Scizzorman C could react to this attack, Paperboy grabbed his scissor gun and punched him to the floor.

Scizzorman A tripped Paperboy, forcing him to drop the scissor gun. He picked up the scissor gun, took out his own scissor gun, aimed both weapons and fired. Paperboy dodged one scissor, but not the other. The scissor hit him. Before Paperboy could react, Scizzorman B tackled him to the floor.

He then got up, took out his scissor gun and aimed. He tossed the other gun to Scizzorman C and he also aimed at Paperboy. Paperboy knew he could not dodge all the scissors. But before any of the Scizzormen fired, someone grabbed Scizzorman A from behind. He fell to the floor. Scott emerged in back of Scizzorman A. He grabbed Scizzorman A's feet and swung him to Scizzorman B and C. Suddenly a key fell out of Scizzorman C's pocket. Paperboy quickly grabbed the key and opened the door the Scizzormen had been guarding. He saw James and Nina tied to a rope that was attached to the wall. James saw Paperboy first.

"Michael!" he exclaimed. Nina looked at Paperboy.

"Took you long enough," she said flatly. She then smiled. "It's good to see you."

"I'll get you out of here," Paperboy announced. Paperboy untied James and Nina from the wall.

"Are you okay?" Paperboy asked.

"We'll be okay," James replied.

"Did they hurt you?" Nina looked at Paperboy.

"Rough night. Let's just leave it at that," she replied.

Paperboy, James and Nina walked out of the room. Outside, Scott threw a scissor gun at Scizzorman C. Scizzorman C fell to the floor. Scott looked at James and Nina. He then tossed a protractor to James and the water pen to Nina. James and Nina were surprised to see him.

"How did ——"

"I'll explain later," Scott interrupted. "We have to leave right now."

Paperboy, James and Nina ran to the stairway. Scott, James and Nina went up the stairway. Paperboy started to go up then he stopped. His conscience would not allow him to go up the stairway.

"Wait," Paperboy said.

Scott turned to him.

"Scott! Leave with James and Nina," Paperboy ordered. "I have something else to do here."

"Are you crazy?" Scott exclaimed. "You're going to be caught."

"I won't be caught," Paperboy argued.

"Why are you staying here?" Scott asked.

"I have to do something. Something that was not part of the plan."

"What do you have to do ?" Scott asked.

" I ——"

"Michael." Scott said. "You can tell me." Paperboy looked at Scott. " It's a long story," he answered. " We don't have time. Just get James and Nina out of here."

"Are you sure?"

"I'm sure."

Scott looked at Paperboy. He then reluctantly went to the stairway, leaving Paperboy in the basement.

"It's time to make things right," Paperboy said bravely.

Chapter 9
The Great Escape

NINE

Paperboy looked around the basement. All the bullies Scott had defeated remained on the ground. Paperboy sighed. He did not want to be here. He wanted to escape with his friends. But Paperboy had to look beyond what he wanted. He had to do what he strongly felt in his heart must be done. Paperboy walked to what he considered was the middle of the basement.

"John!" Paperboy called. No answer. "John," Paperboy called once again.

"Don't hurt me!" a weak voice replied.

Paperboy followed the voice to a door. He then reached down to the bully who had been guarding the door. He pulled a key out of the bully's pocket and opened the door.

"Don't hurt me," John pleaded. "Please?" John started crying uncontrollably.

"I'm not here to hurt you." Paperboy said, tears coming to his eyes.

"Please!" John cried, ignoring Paperboy. "I can't take it anymore. Please don't hurt me."

"I'm not here to ——"

John then started sobbing loudly.

"John!" Paperboy shouted.

John quieted down. For the first time he looked at Paperboy.

"It's you," John said in horror. " You defeated me in the tournament. What do you want from me now?"

"I want to save you," Paperboy answered. "Ever since I defeated you in the tournament, ever since I knew that I sent you back here, I could not forget you, John. I could not sleep. I had nightmares about what they were doing to you. I could not stop thinking about the fact that I, I put you here. You tried to save yourself, you tried to be brave. And I smashed your dreams. I could not live with myself. I could not possible enjoy my life when I know you were forced to live yours here. That's why I'm here. I'm here to make things right. I'm here to rescue you."

"Really?" John asked. Paperboy nodded.

John ran to Paperboy and hugged him.

"Thank you. Thank you so much." John started crying again. But these were not tears of worry or tears of pain. These were tears of hope. These were tears of joy. John then turned around. He looked at the room. This was the room he had experienced a sizable amount of sadness. But now it was over. He was leaving, never to come back again.

"Are you ready to go?" Paperboy asked.

"Yes," John replied. "I'm more than ready."

Meanwhile Scott, James and Nina carefully walked through a hallway.

"Where is Michael?" Nina asked.

"He's …….. He said he had to do something," Scott replied. "I don't know what is was. But it must have been important."

"I hope he's okay," James said.

"Me too," Scott answered.

Suddenly, Scott heard footsteps behind him. He quickly turned around. He saw nothing. Nina and James also turned around.

"What is it?" Nina asked. Scott looked down the hallway.

"Nothing. Let's just get out of here." Scott turned around. Suddenly, a scissor hit Scott on his head.

"Owwww," Scott reacted. He rubbed his head and turned around. Shorty Scarface stood before him.

"I found you," Shorty said in an evil tone. "Destroy James and Nina," he shouted. "Bring Scott to me."

Suddenly, numerous amounts of bullies appeared around the corner in back of Scott, James and Nina. The bullies ran towards the three escapees.

"Run!" Scott ordered.

Scott, James and Nina ran as fast as they could. They turned a corner only to find an army of bullies charging towards them.

"We're trapped," James exclaimed.

"No bully is going to touch me," Nina said defiantly.

Nina fired her weapon at a bully. A pressurized blast of water escaped from the pen and splashed on the bully. The bully fell to the floor. James attacked a bully with his protractors. He then tripped the bully. Scott turned around. To his horror, the bullies they tried to run away from had caught up with them. The bullies charged Scott, James and Nina.

"We're in trouble," Scott whispered.

Meanwhile, Paperboy and John had just ran up the stairway. Paperboy opened the door and stepped out. John then stepped out.

"Do you know how to get to the entrance?" Paperboy asked.

"Yes," John replied.

"Lead the way," Paperboy ordered. John smiled and led Paperboy down two hallways. They turned corner after corner, hallway after hallway.

"Oh!" John gasped.

Paperboy looked at what John had gasped at. Numerous amounts of bullies seemed to be attacking someone. But Paperboy could not see who they were attacking. *It seemed like for every ant that lived on earth, there were two bullies down the hallway.*

"They seem to be attacking someone," Paperboy whispered. He then shivered. "Oh no". He turned to John. "Stay here. When it's safe I'll call you."

"Good luck," John whispered. Paperboy nodded and ran out to face the bullies.

Meanwhile Scott, James and Nina were getting weary. They had managed not to become overwhelmed by the bullies so far. But they were really getting tired. Scott grabbed a bully and swung him into ten other bullies. Suddenly, a bully behind Scott grabbed him. Before Scott could react, another bully ran to him and punched him with all his might. The bully that grabbed Scott slammed him into the floor.

"Scott!" James called.

Forgetting about the bullies, James skated towards Scott. But before he could get there, a bully tackled him to the ground. Nina tried her best to hold her ground. She fired her water pen at a bully and tripped another bully. Suddenly, a bully grabbed Nina from behind.

Another bully prepared to punch her. But before he could, he was attacked by a paper airplane. Nina then freed herself and tripped the bully. She spotted Paperboy close to her. Nina smiled and attacked a bully with her water pen. Paperboy attacked another bully with his paper airplane and moved behind Nina.

"I thought of a way to get all of you out. Tell James and Scott to follow me. You follow me too."

Nina nodded and tripped another bully. "I'll try," she answered. Nina spotted James and called to him.

"James," Nina called. "Follow me."

James who was back on his feet, nodded and followed Nina. Nina attacked a bully with her water pen and searched for Scott. She then saw two bullies carrying Scott. Nina watched as the bullies carried Scott away. Suddenly, Scott pierced a bully with his paper claw and threw the bully into another bully. He fell to his knees. Nina spotted Paperboy and started following him.

James followed her. She ran to Scott, helped him up, and continued following Paperboy. When they were at the end of the hallway, Paperboy ran behind a corner. Nina, James and Scott did the same. They met up with Paperboy and John.

"I'll distract them," Paperboy whispered. "You can then escape the school."

"Who's he?" Scott asked pointing to John. Paperboy ignored Scott and ran back out the hallway. To his delight, he saw the bullies were all confused.

"Hey!" Paperboy shouted. The bullies turned to face him. "Looking for us?" he asked. The bullies ran to Paperboy. Paperboy ran as fast as he could back down the hallway. He turned the other corner without John, Scott, James and Nina and waited. The bullies spotted Paperboy. Paperboy ran down the hallway, the bullies chasing him.

"Be careful!" John called out to Paperboy. Suddenly, some bullies turned to face John, James, Nina and Scott.

"Oh no," Scott whispered.

"They're over here!" the bullies roared. The rest of the bullies turned around and ran to the escapees. Scott, James, John and Nina ran as fast as they could down the hallway. Paperboy watched as the bullies chased his friends.

Scott, James, Nina and John turned a corner. They then saw the entrance to the school. Scott, James, Nina and John ran to the entrance, the bullies in close pursuit. Suddenly, John tripped. A bully grabbed him. James saw this. James threw a protractor at the bully. The protractor hit the bully and he fell. The protractor fell to the floor. Scott opened the door to PS 244 and ran outside. Nina ran outside and grabbed the door. With the bullies less than a foot away from James, James dove out the door. Nina then closed the door.

"No!" James shouted. "That kid.......he did not make it out"

"Neither did Michael," Nina answered.

"My school," Scott said sadly. "What have they done to my school?"

"Let's go," Nina suggested. "We can't go back in and we can't linger here."

"She's right," James agreed. "I just hope Michael is okay. Let's go." Reluctantly, Scott, James, and Nina walked away from PS 244.

CHAPTER 10

PAPERBOY VS. PAPERBOY

Paperboy sighed in relief. John and all his friends were safe. Now Paperboy had to get out of PS 244. Paperboy carefully walked down the hallway. He turned a corner. He saw the army of bullies that had chased John and his friends. The bullies were talking to each other. Paperboy listened keenly and managed to stay out of sight.

"What are we going to do now?" a bully asked.

"Somebody has to tell Shorty Scarface."

"I'll tell him," another bully suggested.

"I'll go with you," another bully said.

"What about him?" a bully asked. The bully pulled up a boy from the floor and held him up. Paperboy's eyes widened. It was John!

"What's your name?" the bully shook John violently.

"I...........I'm J.....ohn," John replied sadly. The bully looked at John.

"You're a prisoner, aren't you?"

"Not anymore." John replied boldly. The bully laughed.

"Sorry, John. You didn't make it out. But don't worry. I'll make sure you pay for trying to escape." The bully looked at two other bullies.

"Take him back to the basement." he ordered. The bullies nodded and grabbed John.

"No!" John shouted. "I can't go back. Help me! Paperboy!" John shouted as the bullies carried him back to the basement.

Paperboy stared at the bullies angrily. He would have helped John but there were too many bullies surrounding him. Two other bullies then walked to the principal's office. The rest of the bullies walked away from the entrance door and back to what they were previously doing. Paperboy looked at the door. All he had to do was open the door and leave PS 244. Nobody was here to stop him. But Paperboy knew what he had to do. He sighed.

"Back to the basement," Paperboy said in a sad tone.

With all the bullies gone, Paperboy retraced his steps to the basement.

The two bullies reached the principal's office door and stepped in. Inside were Shorty Scarface and Copycat. Shorty turned to face the bullies.

"They ….they got away," one of the bullies reported.

"What?" Shorty asked angrily.

"James, Nina and Scott got away," the bully said sadly.

"What about Paperboy?" Copycat asked.

"I saw him in the hallway, where we were trying to capture Scott, James and Nina. But I did not see him escape." The bully turned to the other bully for confirmation. The other bully nodded.

" Paperboy did not escape," he said flatly.

Before Shorty had a chance to think about the situation, Copycat grabbed his knapsack.

"Good," he said. " This time he won't get away."

"What are you going to do?" Shorty asked.

"I'm going to destroy him," Copycat answered. " But this time I won't fail. I've got the perfect disguise." Copycat prepared to walk out of the principal's office.

"Jason. Don't fail me," Shorty said threatening. Jason just smiled confidently and exited the principal's office.

Paperboy stood at the basement door wondering if he was doing the right thing. Paperboy shook his head and opened the basement door. He found the stairway and went downstairs to the basement. Once he was downstairs he heard John.

"No! I won't go back! I can't go back!" John screamed. One bully held John as the other searched the floor.

"Where is the key to his room?" the bully asked loudly.

Paperboy dug into his pockets. He smiled once he felt the key. Paperboy then charged at the bullies. The bully who was not holding John faced Paperboy. But before he could do anything, Paperboy attacked him with his paper airplane. The bully fell to the ground. The bully who was holding John threw John to Paperboy. Paperboy caught him and placed him on the floor. The bully charged. Once he was close enough, the bully tried to punch Paperboy. Paperboy dodged the attack and attacked the bully with his paper airplanes. The bully fell to the ground.

"Are you okay?" Paperboy asked.

"Yes," John replied. Paperboy smiled.

"Let's go. This time nobody will be there to stop us." John nodded. Paperboy and John walked up the stairway. They opened the door and stepped out. Paperboy and John started to walk to the entrance of PS 244. They walked down two hallways. They turned a corner and went down a third hallway. They turned the corner once again. They then saw the entrance to PS 244. Paperboy and John continued walking. Once they were in the middle of the entrance hallway, John spotted a protractor on the floor. Suddenly, a protractor hit John on his head.

"OHHHHHH," John cried as he fell to his knees; while rubbing his head.

Paperboy turned around. What he saw made his eyes widen in surprise. Before Paperboy stood Paperboy! He had all of Paperboy's features and all of his weapons. John looked behind him, then in front of him in confusion. Copycat walked toward Paperboy.

"Too bad, Paperboy," Copycat said. "You could have escaped. You could have escaped PS 244. You could have escaped me."

"I could have escaped," Paperboy replied. "But I came back for him." Paperboy said pointing to John. Copycat looked at John. He laughed.

"You decided to escape with one of our prisoners? You could have left the school but you came back for him?" Copycat chuckled.

"Both of you are going to regret ever messing with LOEP!" With that Copycat charged at Paperboy. Once he was within reach, Copycat attacked with his paper airplane. Paperboy dodged the attack and attacked with his paper airplanes. Copycat dodged the attack and grabbed Paperboy with his paper claw. He swung Paperboy to a nearby wall. Paperboy bounced off the wall. But before he could fall, Copycat grabbed him with his paper claw and pushed him into the wall again.

Using his paper claw, Copycat held Paperboy up against the wall.

"You broke my winning streak. You foiled my plan. And now you are trying to escape with a prisoner of PS 244?"

Copycat threw Paperboy to another wall. Paperboy hit the wall, bounced off and fell to the floor. Copycat picked him up and prepared to attack. Suddenly, Paperboy pierced Copycat's hand with a paper claw. He then attacked Copycat with his paper airplanes.

"AHHHHHHHHHH!" Copycat cried out in pain. Paperboy grabbed Copycat with his paper claw and threw him to a wall. Before Copycat hit the wall, Paperboy threw a PBB at him. The PBB hit Copycat. Copycat hit the wall, bounced off and fell to the floor. Paperboy looked down on Copycat.

"You turned into my friend. You almost made me attack my own brother. And now you turn into me?"

Copycat smiled. He got up and tripped Paperboy. He noticed John three feet away from the battle. He also noticed two protractors on the floor. Copycat's smile grew bigger. Suddenly, Paperboy grabbed him with his paper claw. Before Copycat could react, Paperboy swung him to a nearby wall. Copycat hit the wall, bounced off and hit the floor. While on the floor, Copycat secretly set up a protractor trap. He quickly stood up and tackled Paperboy to the ground. He got up, picked Paperboy up and threw him into the protractor trap. Copycat smiled. Once Paperboy was in the trap he could do whatever he wanted with Paperboy. *Copycat smiled at the thought of throwing Paperboy off the roof of PS 244.* But before Paperboy fell in the trap, John ran to him and pushed him out of the way of it. Copycat watched angrily as Paperboy fell beside him.

"OHHHHHHH," Paperboy groaned.

Paperboy tried to stand up. Copycat fired a PBB at him. Paperboy fell back to the floor. Copycat then turned to John and fired a PBB at him.

"OHHHHHHHH," John cried out in pain. He fell to his knees.

"Never interrupt me again!" Copycat warned. Suddenly, Paperboy got up and attacked Copycat fiercely with his paper airplanes. He spotted the protractor trap, grabbed Copycat with his paper claw and threw him into the trap. Using all of his remaining strength, John pushed Copycat out of the way of the protractor trap. Copycat landed beside Paperboy.

"What are you doing?" Paperboy asked angrily.

"Are you Paperboy? Sorry. I don't know who's who anymore." John replied.

Copycat stood up and grabbed Paperboy with his paper claw. Using all of his strength, Paperboy broke away from Copycat and backed up. Before Copycat could react, Paperboy took out his paper laser and fired.

"AHHHH," Copycat cried out in pain. He moved back a little. Then a little more.

Slowly, Paperboy was pushing Copycat into the protractor trap. When Copycat was an inch from the trap, he noticed this fact. Ignoring the paper ball, Copycat took out his paper laser and fired. The balls from Paperboy's paper laser and Copycat's paper laser hit each other, then they fell to the floor. Neither fighter were being hit with any weapons. Paperboy realized his paper laser was currently ineffective. Copycat knew this too. He smiled.

"Give up, Paperboy. I know all your weapons. I know all your moves. You can't beat me. I'm just like you."

"You're nothing like me!" Paperboy shouted.

However, Paperboy knew Copycat was right. He knew all his weapons and how to use them. How could he defeat Copycat? Suddenly, Paperboy had an idea.

"You know all of my moves." Paperboy admitted. "And you know I have a weakness. I go out of my way to save the people I care about, whether I can actually save them or not. But you have a weakness too, Copycat. Your weakness is you copy everybody you see. But you can do nothing when that person changes. You don't look like that person anymore. Copycat, you have copied all my weapons and how I use them. But you can do nothing when I use them a different way."

For the first time, Paperboy threw one of his paper airplanes. Copycat fired his paper laser faster. The paper balls deflected off the paper airplane. The paper airplane still flew towards him.

"No!" Copycat said. He then threw a PBB at the airplane. Paperboy threw his last paper airplane, this time with more strength. Copycat managed to take the paper airplane down with his PBB. He smiled triumphantly at his accomplishment. He noticed the second paper airplane, but was too late to stop it. The paper airplane hit Copycat on his head. Copycat fell backward from the impact right into the protractor trap. The protractor pierced Copycat's foot. Ropes emerged from the protractors and bound Copycat tightly. John looked at Paperboy.

"Is it you?" he asked.

Paperboy turned to John. "Two bullies tried to lock you in the room. I came and saved you."

"It is you," John replied. He turned to Copycat. " What should we do with him?"

Paperboy thought about this. He then had an idea. Paperboy grabbed Copycat. "Follow me!" he ordered.

Paperboy dragged Copycat all the way to the basement. He carried Copycat down the stairway and into John's former room. He left Copycat in the room, closed the door and locked it with the key. John smiled. Paperboy and John finally exited the basement, ran through the hallways, and finally exited PS 244. Once outside, John looked up at the sky that he hadn't seen in five months as a free person.

"Thank you," John said gratefully. "How can I ever repay you?"

"You don't need –"

"I know," John replied. "If you need anything, just call me and I'll be happy to do it for you." John told Paperboy his telephone number.

"You don't need to do anything for me, John," Paperboy insisted. But John was gone. Paperboy looked around. He smiled as he watched John run down the street screaming, "I'm free! I'm free!"

Paperboy walked home. He took off his mask and cape and walked up to his house.

John reached his house. He knocked on the door. John's mother was in the house. She had given up the searches and all chances of finding her lost son. Ever since John was gone, she could barely eat or sleep. John's mother reluctantly got up and went to answer the door. Once she opened the door, John ran to her. In surprise, John's mother gasped.

She hugged him. John's mother made a silent vow to herself to never again give up hope.

Michael entered his house. His mother was not at home. Michael grabbed the phone and called his brother. Scott picked up the phone.

"Michael?" Scott asked.

"Yeah," Michael answered. Scott sighed in relief.

"You're okay," he said happily.

"How are you?" Michael asked.

"I ....I've been thinking about PS 244. I miss my school. I miss it so much." Scott started making a paper airplane. " I tried to save my school. But I couldn't. Shorty is going to pay. He doesn't know what he's done. And he will never know how much pain he caused me." Scott looked at the paper airplane. "Now I can't even enter the school. Everybody knows me. Everybody knows my face. I just want LOEP to pay for what they have done. But I don't know if I will be the one who makes them pay."

Suddenly an idea came to him. An idea for revenge. Scott hung up the phone. He then colored the finished paper airplane black. He held it up.

"I, Scott, may not be able to save my school, or make LOEP pay for what they have done. But now," Scott said in an evil tone, "I know someone who can!"

Omari Jeremiah:

Omari Jeremiah is a 15-year old African-American teenager from the Bronx, New York. He attended elementary school at CES 109 in the Bronx and middle school at Arturo Toscanni Community Junior High School 145 in the Bronx. He was also a member of the Fieldston Enrichment Program (FEP). This is a program for academically gifted students, which is housed at the Fieldston School in Riverdale, New York. Omari is presently attending the Hackley School in Tarrytown, New York and is in the 10th grade.

Omari has been writing since he was in elementary school. He has written many short stories and poems, His first book, Paperboy, was written when he was only 12 years old and in the 7th grade. He then wrote Paperboy II: Overwhelming Odds when he was 13 years old. These two books have earned Omari a lot of recognition as a talented young author and an inspirational and motivational speaker. He is constantly in demand as a guest speaker at many junior high school graduations and special functions. He has also received many awards for his books. He has been featured in several newspapers across the country and aboard, and has appeared on many radio and television shows.

At age 14, Omari completed the remaining four more books in the Paperboy series. In his third book, Paperboy III: The School of Doom, the talent, humor, imagination, compassion and creativity of this young author are brought to life.

Omari is an avid reader and his other interests include football, tennis, ping-pong and playing the alto saxophone. He wants to be a professional author and saxophonist.

He presently resides in the Bronx with his parents, an older sister and an older brother.

Bernie Rollins:

Bernard (Bernie)Rollins, a California-based artist, designer and art director, created the illustrations for Paperboy III. A New Yorker by birth, from age 5, Bernie drew comic books. When approached by Morton Books with the concept of Paperboy, he remembered his own childhood and drawing comic books at the kitchen table. He felt that helping the author make his story visual was just the way things were supposed to happen.

"It felt right and I had fun doing it," he admits.

Rollins currently works for a Los Angeles newspaper chain.